W9-BWG-313

Song on the Wind

FIFTH HOUSE

written by
CAROLINE EVERSON

illustrated by
ANNE MARIE BOURGEOIS

Published in Canada by Fifth House Publishers,
195 Allstate Parkway, Markham, ON L3R 4T8

Published in the United States by Fifth House Publishers,
311 Washington Street, Brighton, MA 02135

Fifth House Publishers acknowledges with thanks the Canada Council for the
Arts and the Ontario Arts Council for their support of our publishing program.

ONTARIO ARTS COUNCIL
CONSEIL DES ARTS DE L'ONTARIO
an Ontario government agency
un organisme du gouvernement de l'Ontario

Canada Council Conseil des arts
for the Arts du Canada

Library and Archives Canada Cataloguing in Publication
Everson, Caroline, author
Song on the wind / written by Caroline Everson ; illustrated
by Anne Marie Bourgeois. First edition.

Poem.
ISBN 978-1-927083-30-7 (hardcover)

I. Bourgeois, Anne Marie, 1983-, illustrator II. Title.

PS8609.V477S66 2017   jC811'.6   C2017-902208-3 ©

Publisher Cataloging-in-Publication Data (U.S.)

Names: Everson, Caroline, author. | Bourgeois, Anne-Marie, illustrator.
Title: Song On the Wind / written by Caroline Everson ; illustrated by Anne-Marie Bourgeois.
Description: Markham, Ontario : Fifth House Limited, 2017. | Summary: "In Native oral
tradition, a story is told and a song is sung to a sleepy child. The wind carries
it across landscapes, oceans, in time to comfort countless children and send them off to sleep" –
Provided by publisher.
Identifiers: ISBN 978-1-92708-330-7 (hardcover)
Subjects: LCSH: Lullabies -- Juvenile fiction. | Bedtime – Juvenile fiction. | BISAC:
JUVENILE FICTION / Fairy Tales & Folklore / General.
Classification: LCC PZ7.1E947So | DDC [F] – dc23

Cover and interior design by Tanya Montini

Printed in China by Sheck Wah Tong

for Sara, Darren and Tyler
—C.E.

*Thanks to my supportive friends, family
and grandchildren, whose curiosity,
imagination, and belief in magical
possibilities continue to influence my work.*
—A.M. B.

In a long-ago place in a faraway time
A story was sung to the wind.
Lay down your head and I'll tell you a tale
And the wind might catch it again.

As the first of the silver stars blink overhead,
A fading red glow paints the trees.
A sleepy-faced child runs in from her play
And climbs up on her mama's warm knee.

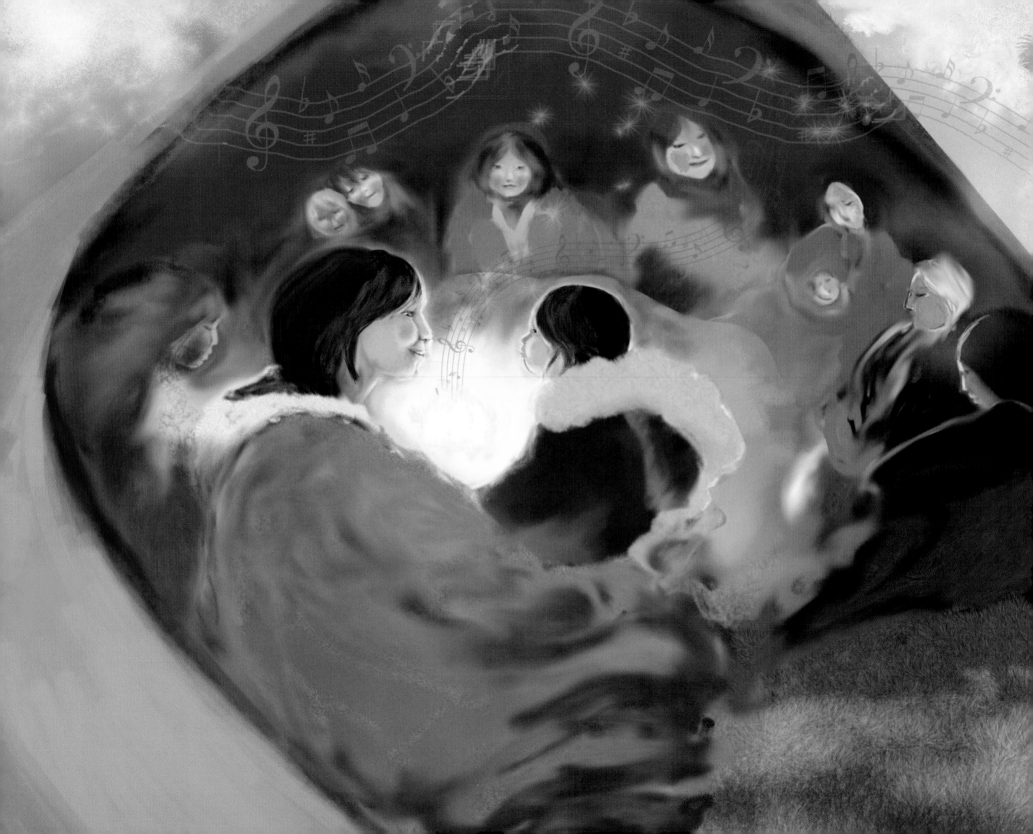

Wrapped in strong arms and soft animal hide,
In the hushed glow of family and fire,
"Mama," she whispers, "please sing me a story
Of water as big as the sky."

Her mama begins…

"In a long-ago place in a faraway time
A story was sung to the wind.
Mama told it to me, and I'll tell it to you,
And the wind might catch it again."

And she sings of the deep and endless sea,
Sleek salmon and gulls wheeling high.
All around and below, a salt-water world
And above the forever sky.

A fishing boat drifts on rippled waves
Washed in orange, vermillion and gold.
The sun sinks low, the colours fade
To periwinkle, violet and mauve.

The fisherman's boy steps into his bunk
And says to his daddy, "Oh, please,
Papa, tell me a story of white bears and igloos,
And ice that covers the sea."

His papa begins...

"In a long-ago place in a faraway time
A story was sung to the wind.
Papa told it to me and I'll tell it to you,
And the wind might catch it again."

And he sings of ice as wide as the sea
Where polar bears hunt fish and seal.
Curtains of colour dance over the sky
Through darkness that lasts half a year.

Fur-wrapped children ride husky-led sleds
Over land held forever in snow.
And at night when the frosty winds blow
   fierce and cold
They gather in snug snow-block homes.

Within the glow of a whale-oil lamp,
A child burrows in for the night.
"Grandmother," she says, "please sing of fast water
And forests where trees reach the sky."

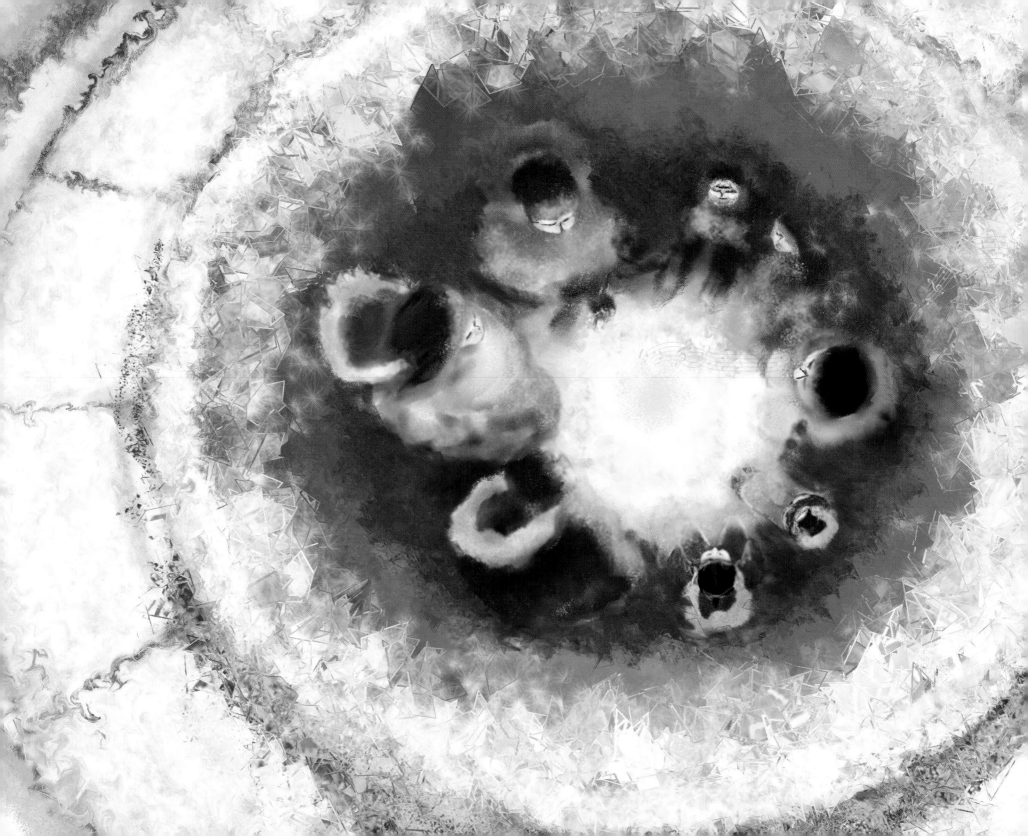

Grandmother begins…
"In a long-ago place and a faraway time
A story was sung to the wind.
Grandmother told it to me and I'll tell it to you,
And the wind might catch it again."

She sings of tall trees as many as fish,
Rivers that flow fast and far.
Circles of stories are sung 'round a fire,
As sparks spiral up to the stars.

In a very close place, in an oh-so-near time,
An old story is sung to the wind.
Lay down your head, my sleepy-eyed child
And the wind might catch it again.